Mr.

by MARGARET EMBRY

Blue

Pictures by BRINTON TURKLE

SCHOLASTIC BOOK SERVICES

Published by Scholastic Book Services, a division
of Scholastic Magazines, Inc., New York, N. Y.

Copyright © 1963 by Holiday House, Inc. This edition is published by Scholastic Book Services, a division of Scholastic Magazines, Inc., by arrangement with Holiday House, Inc.

2nd printing...................................... September 1968

Printed in the U.S.A.

For *Zora*, whose story it was,
and for *Kris*, whose year it was.

Mr. Blue's
Dictionary of Cat Talk

Mr. Blue is a very special cat. He is a Siamese cat. All cats say *meow*. But when a Siamese cat says *meow*, it sounds almost like human words. Mr. Blue can say eight "words." You will read them in this book.

Nank-yu means *Thank you*
Naow means *Meow*
Nn-ee-ow means *Now*
Nn-well means *Well*
Nn-why means *Why*
Nny-out means *Out*
Wow means *Wow!*
Yin means *In*

Miss Zorn's third grade was having reading. The Mountain Lions, the Tigers, and the Panthers had their chairs arranged in three circles around the room. Miss Zorn was helping the Tigers because they usually had the most trouble.

The Panthers were sitting by the long window where the rain was dripping down. Martha was in charge because she was one of the best readers. She called on Tim to read, but all he did was giggle. He was watching a blue cat sitting on the low window sill outside and making faces.

He was a big cross-eyed cat, and he was asking to come in. He was trying to dry himself at the same time. That was impossible, because the rain kept coming down and wetting him more. The window sill was so narrow that he almost fell off.

The Panthers laughed so hard at the way the big cat balanced wobbly on three legs while he stretched the fourth one up like a long turkey drumstick, that Miss Zorn came over to see what the trouble was.

"He wants to come in," Tim said. "Can't we let him in?"

"Certainly not!" Miss Zorn said.

The blue cat heard her. He sat up straight and tall like an old Egyptian stone cat, and looked at the teacher reproachfully with his pale blue cross-eyes.

"Cats don't belong in a schoolroom!"

"Yin!" the cat said quite plainly.

"He said he wants to come in," Martha said. "Didn't you hear him?"

The Mountain Lions and the Tigers crowded around to see what was going on.

"Get back to your seats, boys and girls!" Miss Zorn ordered.

"But he's all wet!" Tim said. "Can't he come in just until he gets dry?"

"Well," said Miss Zorn, "just for a few minutes then."

She went to the outside door and called "Kitty-kitty-kitty!"

The cat jumped down from the sill, but he wasn't

12

in any hurry after all.
He stood in the door
looking all around as
if he were trying to
make up his mind.

"Come on, kitty.
You said you wanted
to come in."

"Nn-well," he said.
And then, "Nn-ee-ow!"

He walked slow-
ly in with great dig-
nity. He explored the

whole room; looked in the closet and in the bookshelves, and at all the children. Then he went to Martha, and jumped on her lap.

"Ooooh! You're all wet, kitty!" She started to push him off, then she said, "Oh, golly, he's so thin. He looks like such a big fat cat, but he's nothing but bones underneath all that fur."

The children came to feel the blue cat's ribs, and their teacher didn't tell them to go sit down.

"He's starving to death!" Tim said.

"Couldn't we feed him, please?" begged Martha.

Miss Zorn frowned, and then she smiled and said, "Tell you what, Martha, you and Tim go down to the Teachers' Lounge and see if there's any coffee cream left in the refrigerator."

The two raced off, each one trying to be the first one there. They were back in a jiffy. Martha set down a saucer, and Tim poured the cream.

14

The cat walked over to see what they had. He didn't rush, but looked around at the children before he started to eat. He was hungry all right, but he didn't gobble or slurp. He drank daintily, and licked the saucer until it shone.

Then he said "Nank-yu!" and walked gracefully over to Miss Zorn's desk. Without asking permission, he sprang up and settled on a stack of arithmetic papers, and began to wash his face.

"Scat!" the teacher said angrily. "You can't sit there!"

The cat looked at her with his eyes narrow. " Nn-why ?" he said loudly.

"Hey, he can talk!" Tim shouted. "Did you hear him? He said, 'Why?' "

"I don't care if he said 'Please!' " Miss Zorn said. "He can't sit on my desk. He's getting my papers all messy."

He jumped down when she gave him a little

16

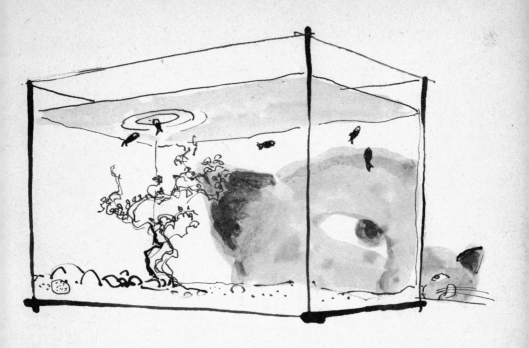

push, and walked over to the long bookcase beside the window. He stood on his hind legs to see how comfortable it was up there.

"No!" yelled the kids. "You can't sit there!"

" Nn-why ?" asked the cat, puzzled.

"The guppies are there," Martha said.

"You'd want to go fishing in the aquarium," Tim giggled.

"Naow!" the cat said, and leaped right up on the shelf.

"Oh, no you don't!" Miss Zorn said, giving him a sharp slap.

"Wow!" he cried, jumping down. Then he went over to a corner to sulk.

Miss Zorn paid him no attention. "Take out your arithmetic books, boys and girls."

The room was quiet except for the rustle of paper, and an occasional sigh when a third grader couldn't remember how many times 3 goes into 21.

Suddenly there was a pitiful cry. It seemed to come from inside the closet, and it sounded as though it might be a little child who was dreadfully hurt.

"Who could that be?" Miss Zorn said.

The closet door was partly ajar. The teacher opened it wider and stepped inside.

Then, "Ouch! You bad, bad kitty!"

The cat ran from the closet, looking for all the world as if he were laughing.

"What happened?" the children asked.

20

"Oh, that cat was hiding there in the dark, and
he pounced on me, and grabbed me around the
ankle."

"Did he bite?" Martha asked anxiously.

Miss Zorn inspected her ankle. "No, he didn't even scratch. He really didn't hurt me at all. He had his claws sheathed. But he surely startled me!"

"I guess he just wanted to play," Martha said.

Tim grinned. "He was probably bored having to sit in the corner while we were all working, and he just wanted to liven things up."

"Well, I'll liven him up if he doesn't look out!" their teacher said. "I'll put him right back out in the rain!"

Annette was waving her hand. "I think we ought to find out who owns him. I could take him around to all the rooms."

"No, I should," Tim said. "I was the one who saw him first."

"But I thought of it first," Annette said tossing her yellow pony tail.

"Nobody will take him," Miss Zorn decided. "It

22

would cause too much disturbance. We'll write a notice instead. What shall we say?"

"Let me write it," Tim said, reaching for his pencil. "Let's see—'Found, Mr. Blue. A big cat with—'"

"Mr. Blue!" Annette scoffed. "What makes you think his name is Mr. Blue?"

"Well, that's as good a name as any—he's blue isn't he?"

"Yes, but you don't know if that's his name or not," Annette said.

"You'd better say, 'Found, big gray-blue cat with cross-eyes,'" Martha said. "And say he can talk too."

"You should add that he can be seen in Room 14," Miss Zorn told him.

Tim wrote it all down carefully. Then he and Annette took the notice around to all of the other rooms. It was nearly lunch time before they were finished.

!! Found !!
A BIG GRAY-BLUE
TALKING CAT
WITH CROSS EYES In ROOM 14

When they got back to their own class there was a crowd of children looking at Mr. Blue. He was sitting on the dictionary table just like a king with his court around him.

A little kindergartner said she thought she knew where he lived. He was too heavy for her to carry, so Tim and Bruce went with her to help.

They came back after lunch still lugging the cat. "He didn't belong there," Tim said, dumping him down in the middle of the floor. "Their cat was gray and white."

24

"Well, what are we going to do?" Miss Zorn asked. "He can't stay here in the school, and scare me half to death every time I go into the closet."

"Nn-why?" Mr. Blue asked impudently.

"Just because, that's why!" Miss Zorn said. "School is really no place for a cat."

But she let him stay anyway. He curled up neatly on the dictionary table, and was no trouble the rest of that day.

The next morning Martha came to school early. She ran down the long flight of steps leading from the parking lot. Mr. Blue walked across the play-

ground to meet her. He was all warm from sitting in the sun, and he felt soft and furry when he rubbed against her legs.

Martha pulled a can of sardines out of her jacket pocket. She opened it with the little key on the top and set it down in front of him.

"Hey, what have you got there?" That was Tim with some other kids.

"Just some breakfast for Mr. Blue," Martha answered.

"He sure does like it," Bruce said.

They watched him lick the can shiny clean, and then he looked up and said something that sounded very much like "Any more?"

"I'll bring you another can tomorrow," Martha promised, "if my mother will let me."

"My mother will let me," Annette said. "I'll bring him a whole can of cat food!"

"I can get him some meat scraps from the store.

The butcher knows me, and he always saves me bones for my dog," Tim said.

Miss Zorn was coming down the steps.

"It won't be hard to feed him if we each take turns," Martha said. "Miss Zorn, can't we keep him for our room pet?"

"Oh, yes," Jean said, jumping up and down. "It would be so much fun. Please!"

"We used to have a guinea pig in first grade," Tim said.

"He wouldn't be much trouble," Bruce said. "We could all take care of him."

Their teacher said that first they must do everything they could to find his owners.

"I've asked everyone I know, and he doesn't seem to belong anywhere," Tim said.

Martha said, "I'll bet he belonged to a family that moved away and forgot him."

"That could be so," Miss Zorn said. "Then you

boys and girls had better start asking your parents to see if you can find a new home for him."

Annette flipped her yellow pony tail excitedly. "I can have him. I know my mother will let me. She says pets are educational."

"If Annette can't have him, maybe I can," Jean said. "I already have a parakeet, but I'd much rather have a cat."

"I'm sure one of you can find a home for him," Miss Zorn said. "Will you be sure to ask at noon?"

They all asked their parents, but they reported to Miss Zorn that all the answers were "No!" Martha's baby sister was allergic to cats, and Tim already had a dog. Jean's mother said the cat would probably kill the parakeet. Bruce's grandma was afraid of cats. Annette said her father had promised to buy her a pedigreed poodle for her birthday and anyone knows that poodles are much smarter than cats.

30

"Oh, I don't know," Tim said. "I don't think an old poodle could talk like Mr. Blue can."

Annette tossed her head. "But a poodle can learn tricks. And you take a poodle walking on a leash."

" Nn-why?" Mr. Blue asked mildly.

The children all howled with laughter, and Tim said, "He says, 'Why? Who wants to go for a walk on a leash anyway?' "

"Oh!" said Annette. "You wouldn't understand!"

Miss Zorn told them to stop their arguing, and they thought she was going to tell them to take out their arithmetic books as she always did when things got noisy. Instead, she said they could start to work on the big social studies mural they were going to make for the hall by the office.

It was going to be about food and shelter. They were going to work on the floor because there weren't any tables in the school long enough.

They pushed all the chairs and desks to one side

of the room, and Miss Zorn unrolled a great long strip of paper that reached almost from one end of the room to the other. It wasn't just ordinary old newsprint like they usually had, but glazed white paper, all smooth and glossy.

Mr. Blue sat on the dictionary table out of the way and watched intently. He didn't pretend to go

to sleep, and he didn't say a thing while Miss Zorn
mixed the paints in some small jars. After she
handed out the brushes, Mr. Blue said " Nn-well!"
and jumped down from the table and came over
for a closer look.

He leaned against Tim's arm. "Nn-well!" he said,
again. Then he patted his paw delicately in the

bright blue sky that Tim was beginning to paint.

"Go away, Mr. Blue!" the boy said, giving him a shove.

The cat jumped and landed right in the middle of the shaggy banana tree Martha was painting.

"Oh, no!" she squealed, and tried to grab him. Annette and Tim reached for him at the same time,

and in the excitement, a jar of black paint was tipped over and ran all across Tim's beautiful sky.

"Oh, golly!" the children cried.

Miss Zorn came hurrying with the sponges and a mop, but it didn't do much good. The mural was ruined.

"Well, at least we had just started," Martha said.

"We can make another one," Tim said.

Miss Zorn's mouth was tight and angry. "I don't know if we can get any more of this kind of paper. The Principal will be very cross when he finds out we ruined this lovely piece he gave us."

35

The boys carried the soggy mural out to the trash can. Miss Zorn finished mopping the floor, and shooed the cat toward the door with the mop.

"Out you go, old cat, and don't you come back!"

"It wasn't his fault," Martha said. "Annette is the one who tipped over the paint."

"I did not!" Annette said. "I bumped into Tim. He spilled it!"

"Well, anyway, Mr. Blue is going out and staying out!" Miss Zorn said. "We just can't work when he's walking around getting into things."

36

She went for more paper, but all they had were short pieces. "We'll have to tape them together when we're done. It won't look as nice, but it will be safer because we can work on the table now."

The children started to work again, this time separately. It wasn't nearly as much fun. Mr. Blue sat on the window sill outside and said, " Yin ! Yin !" until Miss Zorn threw a jar of painting water on him. Then he left and didn't come back.

Mr. Blue wasn't there when the children came to school the next morning. Miss Zorn stood by the window. "He must have found his own family," she said. "I hope they were glad to see him." She was probably a little sorry she had thrown the painting water on him.

At recess that afternoon, the cat came running down the hill from the road to meet the children.

"Mr. Blue's back!" Martha yelled. She picked him up and hugged him. He seemed very glad to see her, and lay all soft in her arms like a big stuffed toy cat.

"Look what I have for you, Mr. Blue," Tim said. He pulled a brown paper packet out of his pocket. The paper was damp and stained. "Look, liver!"

Mr. Blue hopped out of Martha's arms.

"Oh, no, Tim! You haven't carried that in your pocket all day!" Miss Zorn said, shuddering.

"Sure. I knew he'd come back."

The big cat ate the liver eagerly, and said he'd like a little more.

"Sorry," Tim said. "I'll bring you some more tomorrow."

"No, tomorrow's my turn," Annette said. "I haven't had a turn to feed him yet."

"I want to tomorrow," Bruce said. "My Dad and I might go fishing tonight, and I'll save the fish heads to give him."

"My mother said I could bring something for him," Jean said. "She said I could tomorrow."

All the children were talking at once, and then the bell rang, so they never really decided which one of them was going to bring Mr. Blue his food the next day. As it happened none of them did, and he went hungry.

There was a special movie in the auditorium that morning. They all went to it, and forgot and left the cat asleep on the dictionary table. When

they came back, all excited and talking about the movie, Mr. Blue was at the door waiting.

"Nny-out !" he said politely.

"Well, you are a well-behaved fellow today!" Miss Zorn said, opening the door for him.

"Aren't we glad we have him?" Martha said.

Miss Zorn didn't say "yes," but she didn't say

"no" either. She just smiled and told them to get out their pencils and papers.

They were to write a paragraph about the movie they had just seen. Tim had to sharpen his pencil, as he always did when there was any writing to be done. While he was doing it, he leaned over and looked into the aquarium.

"Hey, Miss Zorn! The guppies! They're all gone!"

All the kids got out of their seats and came to see. The aquarium was quite empty of fish.

"Wait a minute," Martha said. "There's one— no, two babies left. See, hiding under the plants."

"But where did the rest of them go?" Jean whispered.

"I can guess. Can't you?" Miss Zorn said.

"Sure," Bruce said. "Mr. Blue ate them."

"Oh, how could he?" Jean gasped, her brown eyes filling with tears.

"Easy—he just fished them out," Tim said. "Just took his paw and scooped them out."

Most of the children giggled, but Annette said, "Well, what a horrid cat!"

"He's not to blame," Martha said, scowling at her. "He didn't have a thing to eat today. What would you do if your stomach was empty, and all those little fish were swimming around just asking to be caught?"

42

"That's right," Miss Zorn said. "He decided if you children forgot him, he'd just have to forage for himself."

"He ate up our poor little daddy guppy with all the lovely red spots on his tail," Jean sniffed, leaning over the aquarium.

"How about those others? The three mamas and all the babies?" Annette said. "Mean old cat!"

Martha shook her red head angrily. "Stop saying, 'Mean old cat!' Cats just naturally like fish. If you had brought him a can of cat food like you promised, he would have left the guppies alone."

"But what are we going to do?" Miss Zorn asked. "Sooner or later he'll catch those other guppies."

Annette's hand shot up. "Let's take him to the Dog Pound."

"He's not a dog, stupid," Bruce said.

"Well, they take stray cats, too, that don't belong anywhere."

"But Mr. Blue's our cat," Tim said. "He adopted us."

"Let's give the aquarium away to Miss Nelson's second grade. They don't have any pets," Martha suggested.

Their teacher looked at them seriously. "Well, what about it?" She knew how much they had enjoyed having the guppies, feeding them, and watching the babies being born and growing up.

Nobody said anything for a while, and then Bruce said, "If we can't keep both, let's give the guppies away. Mr. Blue is more fun. He can talk."

They voted on it. Every hand went up except Annette's.

"Bruce and I will carry it in," Tim said. "Come on."

"Wait a minute," their teacher said. "First Annette had better go ask Miss Nelson if they have room for an aquarium."

The pout on Annette's face faded magically. She was gone only a minute, and came back to report that the second graders were delighted.

Miss Zorn ladled some of the water out of the aquarium so it wouldn't slop over, and Tim and Bruce each took an end very carefully.

While they were gone, Martha said, "Why don't we make a schedule on the blackboard like we did for feeding the guppies, so we'll know who is responsible for feeding Mr. Blue?"

"A very good idea, Martha," Miss Zorn said. She got out her yardstick, and began to rule off lines for names and dates. Each boy and girl would have a turn for one day to see that Mr. Blue was fed and let outside.

Everything went very smoothly until Miss Pettit came Friday afternoon.

Miss Pettit was the music teacher. She came once a week with her wide happy smile and her little pitch pipe. She knew lots of songs, but most of them sounded like kindergarten baby tunes.

Miss Zorn always went to the Teachers' Lounge when it was time for music. She said she needed a little change.

Mr. Blue went in the closet when Miss Pettit came. He didn't say a word, and they all hoped he had gone to sleep. When they started to sing the skipping song that Miss Pettit liked so much, she cried, "No! No! That's not the way it goes at all!"

She made them be quiet while she sang, and her voice was high and shrill. Mr. Blue started to sing too. He started with a moan and ended with a loud wail of pain.

Miss Pettit's eyes got round and startled-looking. "My stars, what is that?"

The children just sat,

hoping Mr. Blue would shush. Even Annette, whose hand was usually waving, was very quiet. Mr. Blue gave another wail.

Miss Pettit pulled the closet door open wider, but she couldn't see a thing. "Who is in there?" Then she stepped inside.

The kids were holding themselves tight to keep the laughter from coming out. They knew what would happen, and it did.

Mr. Blue grabbed Miss Pettit playfully around the ankle. She shrieked, and kicked him with her other foot as she tried to shake him loose. He  kicked with his hind feet like a rabbit, and hung on stubbornly with teeth and claws. When he finally let go, there was blood on her leg, and she was crying.

Miss Zorn and the Principal came running. They took Miss Pettit off to the Nurse's office for first aid.

Then Miss Zorn put Mr. Blue outside. His tail was lashing, and his ears were laid flat back. She told the children to put away their music books and get out their arithmetics.

After a while Miss Zorn said she needed to go down to see how poor Miss Pettit was. She left Martha in charge of the room. Usually when she went out and left them alone for more than a few minutes, some of the boys would begin to throw paper wads, or some of the girls would run up to write on the blackboard. But today, they all sat as quiet and waiting as rows of tenpins.

When Miss Zorn came back her face was very worried. "They had to take poor Miss Pettit home. She has a bite and scratches on her ankle, and she's quite upset. They phoned the man from the Pound to come and get Mr. Blue."

"Oh, no!" the children moaned.

"It wasn't his fault," Martha cried. "Really it wasn't. He was just playing. Just like he always does."

"If she hadn't kicked him—" Tim began.

"I know it wasn't all his fault," Miss Zorn said. "But the school nurse thinks there may be a chance of rabies. He'll have to be held in quarantine."

Annette waved her hand frantically. "He doesn't

have rabies. I know he doesn't. Just dogs can have rabies, and they run around in circles, and blow soap bubbles."

"Cats can carry rabies too," Miss Zorn told them. "Sometimes even field mice or bats have rabies if they've been bitten by some other animal that already has it."

"But Mr. Blue doesn't have rabies. Nothing's bitten him," Martha said.

"We don't know for sure, Martha, so it's better that he goes to the Pound where they can watch him. Rabies is a very serious disease."

"What will they do with him there?" Jean asked fearfully.

"They'll keep him quiet for a week or so, and then if he doesn't show any symptoms maybe they'll let him go."

"But if nobody comes to claim him they'll put him to sleep," Annette said.

"Then we'd all better try to find a home for him, hadn't we?" Miss Zorn said. "Now, let's get back to work. Tim, did you get the answer for that first arithmetic problem?"

It was one of those story problems, and it was long and hard. While Tim was explaining how much four pieces of bubble gum at two for a penny plus six suckers at three for a nickel plus two candy bars at ten cents each would cost, someone knocked on the hall door.

It was a man in white coveralls. He said he was from the Pound and had come to get the cat that was causing Trouble.

"Oh, dear," Miss Zorn said. "He's not here. We put him outside."

"You mean you turned him loose?" the man asked, astonished. "He might bite someone else!"

"He won't unless someone kicks him again," Tim said.

"I'm sure he doesn't have rabies," Miss Zorn said. "He just got upset, and I thought it was better that he be put outside."

"Well somebody'd better find him quick," the man said.

Annette's hand was up like a flash. "I will! Let me go!"

"Tim and Martha had better go look," Miss Zorn decided. "He's most likely to come to them."

The two children walked all around the school, across the playground, and up the steps to the parking lot, calling "Kitty-kitty-kitty!" but they couldn't find him anywhere.

"You know what, Tim?" Martha said. "I hope we can't find him."

"Me too," Tim said. And he began calling more and more softly.

Then suddenly something grabbed Tim around the ankle. He reached down and picked up Mr. Blue. He shook him a little. "Why did you do that, you crazy old cat? Don't you know there's a price on your head? Why didn't you go into hiding?"

"We have to take him back," Martha said. "The Pound Man is waiting for him."

"I don't care," Tim said, setting him down. "Go away, Mr. Blue! Scat!"

But Mr. Blue stood there staring up at the children with his puzzled cross-eyes and wouldn't move. Then they heard Miss Zorn calling them, and saw the Pound Man coming up the steps to meet them.

"Here now, I'll take that fellow!" the man said, reaching for Mr. Blue.

Mr. Blue didn't like the looks of the Pound Man. He didn't like the smell of his coveralls, which probably had Dog all over them. He laid back his ears and growled.

"Maybe you'd better let me take him for you," Martha said.

She carried him over to the white Pound truck. Mr. Blue kept his paws tight around Martha's neck, and looked sadly over her shoulder at Tim. The

man opened a cage in the back of the truck. Martha put Mr. Blue in, but it was hard to make him let loose.

The man put a padlock on the cage. "Be good to him," Martha said. "He's really a very gentle cat if you're good to him."

"Sure," said the man. "Don't worry!"

They watched him drive off, and they both waved to Mr. Blue, who was looking out the back of the truck unhappily.

"A week sure is a long long time!" Tim said.

Friday finally came, and the children were out on the playground for afternoon recess. Tim was playing kickball with the other boys, and Martha was swinging when she saw Mr. Blue come daintily down the long flight of stairs from the parking lot.

She jumped out of the swing while it was still moving, and ran to swoop him up in her arms.

"Mr. Blue's back!" she cried to the other kids. "They must have turned him loose!"

"I'll bet he chewed his way out!" Bruce said.

"Well, he's still supposed to be in quarantine," Annette said. "They probably don't know he's gone."

"Aw, they do too," Tim said. "Today's Friday, and it's been a week. The man said he only had to stay a week or so."

Annette flipped her pony tail. "They wouldn't just turn him loose, silly. I'm going to tell Miss Zorn and have her call the Pound. I'll bet he ran away."

"Old Tattle-tale!" Tim shouted at her back, as she flounced into the schoolroom.

Annette was right. In a few minutes Miss Zorn came out to tell them that Mr. Blue had escaped while they were cleaning the cages, and the Pound Man would be right over to see about him.

"Tim, you and Martha stay out here and watch

Mr. Blue until the Pound Man gets here. It's time
for the rest of you boys and girls to come inside."

"Aw, can't we stay just until the man gets here?"

Bruce beggged. "Please, can't we Miss Zorn?"

"Recess is over," Miss Zorn said. "Inside, all of you. It's almost time for Miss Pettit to come."

The other children went in with their teacher. Martha sat in the swing holding Mr. Blue on her lap. Tim stood beside her petting him.

"You sure made a good try," Tim said rubbing the big cat's ears. "And you knew just where to come, too."

"He's a smart cat," Martha said. "He knows where his home is."

"If it weren't for that old Miss Pettit, we could keep him," Tim said.

Mr. Blue purred loudly and twisted his head so Tim could scratch under his chin.

"Here comes Miss Pettit now," Martha said.

They watched the music teacher park her little black car in the lot above them. She climbed out, banged the door, and started down the steps swinging her little music case.

"She doesn't look very hurt," Tim said. "I can't see even one little old scratch."

62

Miss Pettit's wide happy smile faded when she saw Mr. Blue. "What are you children doing with that dreadful animal?"

"We're taking care of him for Miss Zorn," Tim said.

"Well, he's supposed to be in the Dog Pound," Miss Pettit said. "He's dangerous to have around."

"He's not dangerous at all," Martha said. "He's a very loving cat."

64

"Loving!" Miss Pettit said. "My stars, child, did you see how he attacked me?"

"He didn't mean to hurt you, honest!" Martha said. "He was just playing a little."

"Sure," Tim said. "He grabs me around the ankle all the time, don't you, Mr. Blue? But he hates to be kicked back."

Just then another car was being parked in the lot above them. It was the white Pound truck.

"Oh, golly!" Martha said. "Here he comes now."

"Here who comes?" Miss Pettit said.

"The Pound Man," Tim said. "He's come to get Mr. Blue. If you weren't so scared of him, maybe we could keep him."

Miss Pettit started to say something, but the Pound Man came hurrying down the steps. He had on heavy gloves, and he reached out for the cat.

"I should have guessed he'd be here!" he said.

Mr. Blue laid back his ears and gave a snarl. He leaped right out of Martha's arms and landed on Miss Pettit, who dropped her music case in surprise. He put his paws around her neck.

"Well!" Miss Pettit said, looking a little pleased. She started to put her arms around him, but he gave a wild cry and jumped again, right over her shoulder.

They all looked up then, and saw the white Pound truck rolling right toward them down the

66

steep slope, mowing down all the small bushes as it came. For a minute they couldn't seem to move, until Mr. Blue gave another wild cry.

"Run!" yelled the Pound Man. Miss Pettit pushed Tim and Martha out of the way, and fell on top of them. The man tried to grab for the truck to stop it, but it was going too fast.

It bumped past them and knocked the swings over. Then it crashed into the wall of the school.

"Mr. Blue!" Tim yelled. "What happened to Mr. Blue?"

He and Martha scrambled to their feet and started to run up the slope. They could hear people coming out of the school, shouting and asking what had happened. They could hear Miss Zorn calling their names, but they had to find Mr. Blue.

They ran through the parking lot, up the road to the highway, and there he was on the other side, sitting on the guard rail, calmly washing his face.

"Well," gasped Martha, her freckles standing out like red buttons. "At least he wasn't hurt."

"Aw, he's too smart to get hurt," Tim said. "Come on, fellow."

"Let's just leave him here," Martha said. "Maybe he'll run away, and won't have to go back to that old Pound."

"He won't run away," Tim said. "He belongs to us. They'll have to let us keep him now because he saved our lives. If he hadn't yelled we might never have seen that old truck in time."

69

That's exactly what the Principal said when he heard the whole story. He said Mr. Blue was a very remarkable cat and had certainly earned his place

as a member of Miss Zorn's third grade, if the Pound Man would turn him loose.

The Pound Man looked at his watch and said the quarantine was over at exactly 3:30 p.m. Since Mr. Blue had shown no signs of rabies, and he had a good home promised him, he could be set free.

71

Miss Zorn said, "But what about Miss Pettit and the Friday music hour?"

Miss Pettit reached out and patted Mr. Blue's head gingerly. "Oh, I think we will manage. He can sing right along with us. He has a most interesting voice."

Mr. Blue, lying back in Martha's arms like a floppy old stuffed cat, smiled. " Nank-yu ," he said, quite plainly.